A VERY SPECIAL B

Three stories about Lucy Billings, her family and friends, and her life in Codling Village.

Susan Hill is one of Britain's leading writers for both adults and children. Her books for children include another title about Lucy Billing and friends, *Friends Next Door*, as well as *Can It Be True?* (winner of the 6–8 years category of the Smarties Book Prize), *Septimus Honeydew*, *Beware, Beware*, *King of Kings*, *The Christmas Collection* and *The Walker Book of Ghost Stories*. She lives in the Cotswolds, Gloucestershire with her husband and two daughters.

Paul Howard has illustrated a number of stories for Walker, including *Jim's Winter*, *Taking the Cat's Way Home*, *One for Me, One for You*, *Care of Henry* and the picture books *John Joe and the Big Hen*, *Rosie's Fishing Trip* and *A Year in the City*. He is married and lives in London.

Frank showed Lucy and Jane Jones a plant that he had grown himself in his own greenhouse.

STORIES FROM CODLING VILLAGE

A VERY SPECIAL BIRTHDAY

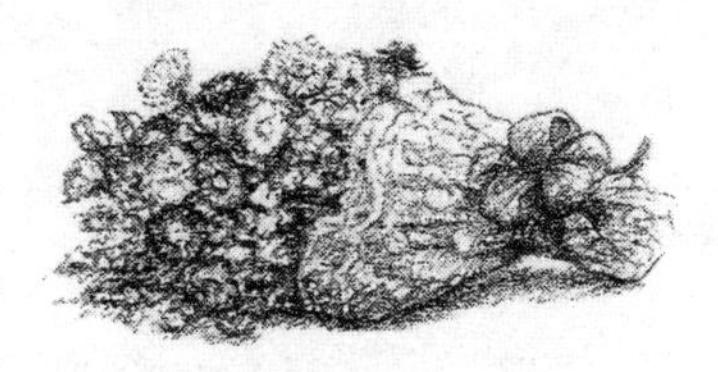

Written by
SUSAN HILL

Illustrations by
PAUL HOWARD

WALKER BOOKS
AND SUBSIDIARIES
LONDON • BOSTON • SYDNEY

First published in Great Britain 1990 by
Julia MacRae Books
This edition published 1992 by Walker Books Ltd
87 Vauxhall Walk
London SE11 5HJ

4 6 8 10 9 7 5 3

This book is typeset in Plantin

Printed in England by
Clays Ltd, St Ives plc

British Library Cataloguing in Publication Data
A catalogue record for this book
is available from the British Library.

ISBN 0-7445-2418-0

CONTENTS

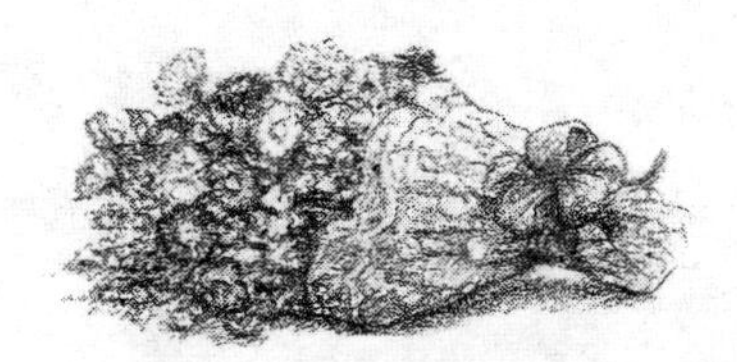

Jane Jones put up her hand.

A VERY SPECIAL BIRTHDAY

At eleven o'clock every morning, Lucy Billings and Jane Jones and all the other children at the Codling Village playgroup, sat down and had a mug of milk to drink and two sugary biscuits. And one fine morning in November, when they were all nicely settled, Mrs Greene, who was the lady in charge, said that she had something special she wanted to talk to them about.

"Now I'm sure that you all know Mrs Tabb, who lives at Number 14, Codling. Is there anyone who *doesn't* know her?"

Jane Jones put up her hand, because she hadn't lived long enough in Codling Village to know many people at all.

"Well," said Mrs Greene, "Mrs Tabb was born in the cottage that she still lives in, the one at the very end of the row, next to the church path, and she was christened in our church and married there too, and all her children and grandchildren were christened and married there."

"Yes," said Lucy Billings, "and Mrs Tabb always sits in her chair by the window in winter, and in her chair in the front doorway when it's summertime."

"And she always waves to me," said Mark-by-the-pond (whose real name was Mark Field, only everybody called him Mark-by-the-pond, because that was where his house was, so as not to mix him up with Mark Cherry, who was called Mark-down-the-lane).

Then the others all said, "Yes, yes," because Mrs Tabb always waved to them, too.

"She waves to everybody," Mrs Greene said. "She is a friend to all the village. And something very special and important is going to happen to Mrs Tabb next Thursday, which is November the sixth." (And Sam Smith interrupted to say that November the sixth was the day after bonfire night, but Mrs Greene said that they would talk about bonfire night another time, because just now they were talking about Mrs Tabb.)

"On November the sixth it is Mrs Tabb's birthday," she said, "and it won't be just an ordinary birthday. Mrs Tabb is going to be ninety years old, and then she will be the oldest person in Codling Village."

She went on to say that because Mrs Tabb was a friend to all the village and to everybody in the playgroup, and because ninety was such a special age to be, they were going to do something special for Mrs Tabb. Next Thursday morning, they were all going to walk along Codling Village High Street, from the village hall, to Mrs Tabb's cottage, and they were going to go up her garden path, and stand under her window, and then they were going to sing to her.

"What will we sing?" asked Mark-by-the-pond.

And Mrs Greene said, "Well, what do *you* think we are going to sing?" and they all shouted "Happy birthday to you!" so loudly that Mrs Greenee had to put her hands over her ears! Then she said that yes, they would certainly sing "Happy birthday to you", and that they would sing another song, too, and the song was called "Bobby Shaftoe", and she told them the first verse. Which was:

Bobby Shaftoe's gone to sea,
Silver buckles on his knee,

He'll come back and marry me,
Bonny Bobby Shaftoe.

"We're going to learn to sing that," Mrs Greene said, "because it is Mrs Tabb's favourite song of all."

And when Lucy Billings asked her why, she said that Mr Tabb, Mrs Tabb's husband, had been a sailor who had gone to sea, and that *he* had been called Bobby.

So then Mrs Greene went to the piano in the corner, and they all gathered round her, and she played the tune of "Bobby Shaftoe" over three times, and then Mrs Wood, who helped her at the playgroup, sang the words. And Jane Jones suddenly said that she knew the song already, she had learned it at her old playgroup, and one or two of the other children knew it, too, so they sang with Mrs Wood.

The playgroup spent a lot of time learning "Bobby Shaftoe" and "Happy Birthday to you".

For the rest of that week, every morning, the playgroup spent quite a lot of time learning to sing "Bobby Shaftoe" and practising "Happy Birthday to you", so that they could go to Mrs Tabb's house and sing the songs to her.

"But will we have to push the piano all the way along to Mrs Tabb's house?" somebody asked, and Mrs Greene and Mrs Wood laughed a lot and said no, it would be much too heavy and awkward.

"Mrs Wood's daughter Kathy will be home from college that week," said Mrs Greene, "and she's going to bring her guitar and play that for you to sing to." Which they all thought was a very nice idea.

And Lucy Billings and Jane Jones practised singing "Happy Birthday to you" and "Bobby Shaftoe" at home, every minute that they could (and so did all the other children at the playgroup) until in the end Lucy's mother said, "Oh, not *again*!" and Jane Jones' mother said, "I think you know them quite well enough by now!" and Lucy Billings' father said, "Change the record, old girl," and Jane Jones' father said, "No wonder Bobby Shaftoe went to sea!"

But Lucy and Jane Jones (and all the other children at the playgroup) said they had to make sure their songs were quite perfect by next Thursday and that was why they had to practise and practise, because Mrs Greene and Mrs Wood had said so.

On the morning of November the sixth, Lucy Billings jumped out of bed and ran to her window and drew back the curtains and clapped her hands for joy, because it was a *beautiful* morning with a bright blue sky, and the sun just coming out, which was exactly right for a special birthday. Though

Mr Billings said that there had been a sharp frost during the night, and all the dahlia flowers had been pinched off by it, and Mrs Billings said that Lucy would have to wrap up really warmly, with her scarf and hat and gloves as well as her coat, because it would be chilly standing outside Mrs Tabb's house while they sang.

When Lucy heard the post van and ran down the front path to the gate to collect the letters from the wooden box, the post lady said that she had a very big pile of letters and cards and parcels indeed for Mrs Tabb's house. And when Frank the milk-man came in his float, whiny whiny rattle-chink down the lane, he showed Lucy and Jane Jones, who were just setting off for the playgroup, a plant that he had grown himself in his own greenhouse and which he was going to give to Mrs Tabb for his present. And Lucy and Jane Jones hoppity-skipped all the way up to the village hall, they were so excited. "Almost as excited as on *my* birthday," Lucy said.

Everybody at the playgroup kept their coats on, and when they had all arrived, Kathy Wood showed them her guitar and played the tunes over to them, to warm up. Then they had one quick practice. Mrs Greene had a posy of dried flowers which she said were best, because there were not very many fresh ones about in November, and besides, Mrs Tabb would be able to keep this posy for always, to remind her of her ninetieth birthday.

And then they set off, two by two in a crocodile, with Mrs Greene at the front and Mrs Wood at the back, and Kathy Wood in the middle with her guitar. On the way they met quite a few people they knew – Frank

And then they set off, two by two in a crocodile.

the milkman again, and Mr Potter the vicar, and people going by in their cars slowed down when they saw them and tooted their horns and smiled and waved.

When they got to Mrs Tabb's house they walked up the path, and first of all Mrs Greene tap-tapped on the brass knocker, and Mrs Tabb's granddaughter, Mrs White, opened the door and she looked very pleased and smiley. But she put her finger to her lips, to show them that they must keep very quiet, because the singing was to be a great surprise. Then she whispered that she would open the front window so that Mrs Tabb would be able to hear them clearly, and while they gathered beneath the window, she went to fetch Mrs Tabb, who was in the kitchen at the back of the cottage, and sat her comfortably in her chair with three cushions around her. Then Mrs

White looked out of the window, and nodded to Mrs Greene, and Kathy Wood went to the front, right under the window, and played the first few notes of music on her guitar. And then everybody began to sing. They sang as clearly and as loudly and as beautifully as they possibly could:

Happy birthday to you.
Happy birthday to you.
Happy birthday, Mrs Tabb,
Happy Birthday to you.

And then, after a little rest, they sang:

Bobby Shaftoe's gone to sea,
Silver buckles on his knee,
He'll come back and marry me,
Bonny Bobby Shaftoe.

And when Lucy Billings looked up, she saw that Mrs Tabb was standing right beside the open window, and leaning on the ledge, so that she could see them all, as well as hear them, and she was smiling and smiling and looking so pleased and so surprised. When they had finished, she clapped her hands a great deal, so they sang "Bobby Shaftoe" all over again. And some people who had come out of the other houses and were standing by their front doors, and some other people who had come down the High Street and were standing on the other side of the wall, all clapped too.

Then Mrs Greene said that they had all come to wish Mrs Tabb a happy birthday and many happy returns of the day, and that they had brought a small gift, and she wanted Lucy Billings, who had been at the

Mrs Tabb was standing right beside the open window.

Codling Village playgroup the longest time of them all, to come up and give the posy of flowers to Mrs Tabb. Only Lucy took Jane Jones' hand and made her come up too, because *she* had been at the playgroup the shortest time and because she was Lucy's friend-next-door.

Then they took the dried flower posy and handed it through the open window and Mrs Tabb said, "Thank you, oh, *thank* you!" and kissed both their hands (because she couldn't reach down far enough to kiss their faces!). And Lucy saw that as well as smiling and being very pleased and surprised indeed, Mrs Tabb's face had some tears on the cheeks – which she knew meant that she was really, really happy!

After that, as they were going away, Mrs Tabb's granddaughter came out of the cottage with a tin of sweets and there was one for each of them "from Gran," Mrs White said. So they all went back down the High Street in the sunshine, sucking their sweets and feeling very happy and pleased, on Mrs Tabb's ninetieth birthday.

In the middle of the orchardy bit was a hen house.

APPLE CHUTNEY

At the bottom of the garden at Beehive Cottage, where Lucy Billings lived, there was an orchardy bit, with apple trees and pear trees growing. In the middle of the orchardy bit was a hen house, and in the hen house lived seven brown hens. Around the hen house was a run made of strong wire netting to keep the foxes out. But there was a gate in the netting and, sometimes, Lucy's mother let her open it, and then the hens would come trotting and cluck-cluck-clucking out, to peck and scratch and strut about in the long grass.

When Lucy was smaller, she had been a bit worried by the hens and afraid that they would peck at her with their hard little yellowy beaks. But she was quite used to them now and not a bit frightened: she took down a panful of corn and scattered it about for them in the afternoons, and helped her mother or father to give them their food, which was called mash, and change their water. She could even carry a small basket down to the hen house and collect the eggs. That was what she loved to do best of all: she loved opening the door and smelling the henny-straw smell. Sometimes, one of the brown hens was sitting in the warm, dark inside of the hen house and made a gentle little cluck from its nesting box when Lucy went in, and she talked back to it in a soft voice. "There, girl," she said, as she had heard her mother do. "There, there, there."

So, one fine afternoon, she was very

pleased indeed when Dr Wilkins called to see if there were some spare eggs that she could buy, and Lucy's mother said that Lucy might take the basket down to the hen house all by herself, and see.

The gate was open, and the hens were outside in the orchardy bit, but they didn't come running up to Lucy, because she had already been to get them their pan of corn just after dinner; they just went on pecking about – though they did look at her with interest, to see what she going to do.

She lifted the latch of the hen house door, and went inside and the straw prickled her ankles and made its nice rustly-scratchy noise. There wasn't a hen on the nest this time, but when Lucy reached down, she found five brown eggs and they were still warm. She picked them up one by one and put them into the basket. She liked the feel of them, they were very smooth and dry and quite heavy.

Then she locked the door again and carried the basket slowly and carefully back to the kitchen, where Dr Wilkins was talking to her mother. She was saying that she had just been to Forge Cottage to see old Mr Bean, who had broken his leg in the summer, and been in hospital. Mr Bean wasn't just old, he was very, very old indeed, and everybody had been very worried when he had fallen going down his garden path, and his leg had been broken quite badly. But Dr Wilkins said he was doing very well indeed now, and his leg was "mending nicely".

"He wants to get it completely right again in time for the Christmas Party," she said. And then, because she could see that Lucy was very interested, Dr Wilkins told them

Lucy carried the basket slowly and carefully back to the kitchen.

that some of the people had decided that it would be a good idea to have a Christmas party especially for all the old ladies and gentlemen who lived in Codling Village. It was to be held in the Village Hall on the Saturday before Christmas, and there would be a proper sit-down Christmas dinner, and then an entertainment, with games and singing.

"They're having Father Christmas, too," Dr Wilkins said, "and everyone will take home a present."

"I think that's a lovely idea," said Lucy's mother, "but won't it cost a lot of money?"

"Yes, and we don't want our guests to have to pay for anything at all, so we're going to try and raise some money. There's to be a jumble sale and Mrs Preston, at the Grange, has said that she will have a Coffee Morning, with a raffle. If you can think of any other ways we might raise some money, just let us know."

And then Dr Wilkins paid for the eggs and said that she had better dash, because she had to collect her twins from the school bus at the crossroads.

"Well," said Lucy's mother, when Dr Wilkins had gone, "I'd better look out something for the jumble sale. There's always something in the cupboards that we don't need any longer, but somebody else might want. Perhaps you and Ben could go through your toy boxes, Lucy, and see if there are any things you don't play with now."

"Yes," said Lucy, "and I'll go and ask Jane Jones and *her* mother." And she ran down the garden and climbed over the open bit of fence into the garden of the house next door.

But Jane Jones' mother said that they didn't really have anything for jumble, because of having only just moved. "We gave everything we cleared out of the old house to the Boy Scouts, for *their* jumble sale," she said, "so I'm not sure what we can do. Can you two think of anything?"

So Lucy and Jane went back down the garden of Old Leas Farmhouse and over the open bit of fence, into the garden of Beehive Cottage, and got into the swings that hung from the apple trees in the orchardy bit, and talked and talked, and swung and swung and thought and thought, until Lucy's mother came down to them, carrying two flat wooden boxes.

"Would you two like to do a helpful job? Will you pick up as many of these windfall apples as you can, and put them into the boxes? They say that it's going to rain later, and once the fallen apples get wet they'll go bad quite quickly."

So Lucy and Jane did. They poked about in the long, tussocky grass under the trees for apples, and laid them in the wooden boxes, being very careful to check that there weren't any wasps crawling on them first, and throwing away any apples that had holes in them, where the tiny maggots had burrowed their way through.

It was very good fun but quite tiring, and after a time, their backs began to ache from all the bending over, and just as they thought they would simply *have* to stop and rest, Lucy's mother called from the kitchen for them to come and have drinks of milk and some biscuits.

And as they sat at the kitchen table, enjoying them, Lucy said, "What are we going to *do* with the apples? There are a lot."

She pretended that the iron was a dragon, with smoke puffing out of its mouth.

"I know," said her mother, and she banged the iron down onto a pair of trousers, and then took it away again very quickly, so that the steam hissed up. (Lucy always enjoyed that – she pretended that the iron was a dragon, with smoke puffing out of its mouth.)

"It's a problem every time we have a good apple year. We can store some of the apples in the loft, but there isn't very much room. I shall make some apple pies and put them in the freezer. But there are always quite a lot left over, and I do hate to waste them. Perhaps I'll just put them in a box by the front gate, with a notice asking passers-by to help themselves."

"I know, we could *sell* them and give the money for the old people's Christmas party!" Lucy said.

But her mother said that although that

was a very kind thought, the trouble was that everybody in Codling Village had too many apples this year. "So nobody would want to buy any of ours."

"What if we *made* them into something, and sold the somethings?"

"Well..."

"Oh, could we, please, *please*?" said Lucy and Jane Jones together.

"What do you think you could make? I don't mind helping a bit but it really ought to be something you can do all by yourselves, oughtn't it? Then it really *would* be your own way of making some money for the Christmas party."

Then they thought about it and thought about it. Apple pies and apple tarts and apple crumble were no good, because Lucy's mother would have to do so much of the work.

"Well, think of all the jobs you *can* do yourselves," Mrs Billings said.

So they thought and thought again, and Lucy's mother got a paper and pencil and wrote down a list of what they had thought and the list said that Lucy Billings and Jane Jones could:

Collect things
Sort things
Wash things
Weigh things
Peel things
Chop things
(being very careful
with sharp knife)
Pour things
Mix things
Spoon things out

And when she read the list out loud, they all looked at one another and said, "*Apple chutney*!"

Then Lucy's mother said that she had a lot of jamjars that she'd been wanting to use for something or other, to make some room in the larder cupboard, and she got out the recipe book and found the recipe for apple chutney, and made *another* list of all the things they would need to make it. This list said:

Apples
Vinegar
Sugar
Onions
Raisins
Ground Ginger
Spice
Salt
Pepper
Lemons

Then Lucy and Jane went looking in the larder and found everything they would need except raisins – there were only two or three left, rolling round the bottom of the jar. But Mrs Billings said that she could do with taking Rosie the baby out for some fresh air. So they all got their coats and boots on, and on the way Jane Jones ran into the house next door, to ask if she might go with them, and to put on *her* coat and boots. Then they walked up the lane and through Codling Village to Mrs Dobby's post office shop, where they bought the raisins and another bag of brown sugar, just in case they ran out. When Mrs Dobby heard about the plans to make apple chutney, she said that if the jars looked really smart, with proper caps and labels on, she would take some to sell in her shop; she said that she would stand them on the counter and prop a special notice beside them, to say who had made the chutney and what the money was

They mixed and mixed and mixed and mixed.

for. She also gave Lucy and Jane Jones and Rosie the baby a white chocolate mouse each, because she said they deserved it for their kindness.

So that afternoon, as soon as dinner was over, Jane Jones came round to Beehive Cottage and while Rosie the baby went down for her nap, Mrs Billings cleared the big kitchen table and the girls washed their hands and put on aprons (and Jane Jones had to borrow one of Lucy's mother's aprons, which was much too big for her and made them laugh, she looked so funny). And then they sorted and weighed and washed and peeled and chopped (being very careful with the sharp knife) and measured out and spooned in and mixed and mixed and mixed and mixed. Mrs Billings scarcely had to help them at all.

By the time they had finished they were

tired and sticky and a bit hot, so they took off their aprons and washed their hands again, and then Lucy's mother said that while she put the chutney onto the stove to cook, they could go out into the garden to play.

So they did. They swung on the swings and then they played galloping horses with broomsticks from the shed. In the kitchen the chutney simmered and bubbled and the sweet-spicy-vinegary-appley smell of it seeped out through the open door, so that when Jane Jones' mother came round with Jack, a bit later, she stopped halfway down the path and said, "*What* is that delicious smell?"

Later, when the chutney had cooked right through and then cooled on the window-ledge, Lucy and Jane Jones spooned it carefully, spoon by spoon, into the gleaming-clean jamjars, and stuck little

They played galloping horses with broomsticks from the shed.

waxy paper circles on the top. And Jane Jones' mother said that if they liked, she would decorate some plain white labels and write

APPLE CHUTNEY
by
Lucy Billings and Jane Jones

on them in her special writing (because she was an artist and could do painting and drawing and decorating with special writing, quite beautifully). Lucy's mother found some spare pieces of red-and-white and blue-and-white cotton material in her sewing drawer and Lucy and Jane Jones drew around big cardboard circles onto the material and then cut them out with the pinking-shears that made frilly edges.

When the red-and-white and blue-and-white material covers were fitted onto the lids of the jars with elastic bands and the decorated and specially-written labels stuck on the front, the rows of chutney jars looked perfect. "Better than in the shops," said Lucy's father, when he came home.

"Yes," said Lucy, "and the chutney tastes better too."

Which everyone in Codling Village who bought it agreed was perfectly true. Because as soon as the jars went onto Mrs Dobby's post office shop counter, she started to sell them. And Lucy and Jane Jones also set up a stall, made out of one of the old packing cases, and covered with a tablecloth, between the front gate of Beehive Cottage and the front gate of the house next door, and Jane Jones' mother wrote out a notice about the chutney, and they propped it up in front of the row of jars.

That day was a Saturday, and the Billings family went off for the whole day to Fairleigh, to have lunch and tea with their cousins, and by the time they got back, it was dark. But there was a huge moon, and when their car stopped beside the front gate, Lucy could see the white tablecloth gleaming on top of the packing case – gleaming, and *empty*!

"It's gone, it's gone!" she said, scrambling out of the car. "All the chutney has been sold!"

"Yes," said her father, picking up the tin box they had left beside it, "the stall is empty, but *this* feels rather full," and he shook it and it rattled and then he gave it to Lucy to carry into the house.

"A lot of people come walking down this way at the weekend, especially when the weather's so fine," said Lucy's mother. "I thought it would be a good day to set up a stall."

Then Lucy poured the money out of the

"All the chutney has been sold!"

tin onto the big kitchen table, and they all agreed that big brother Ben should be the one to count it. So while Mrs Billings was putting Rosie the baby to bed and Mr Billings was putting the potatoes into the oven to bake for supper, Ben Billings counted the money very, very carefully. And he found that there was £11.50. And on Monday, Mrs Dobby said that she had sold out of the apple chutney that she had taken for the shop, and her money came to £6, which made £17.50 altogether.

Then Lucy Billings's mother wrote a letter to Mrs Day at Codling Farm, who was in charge of organizing the Christmas party for the old people, and explained all about the apple chutney that Lucy and Jane Jones had made. She put the letter, with the money inside it, into an envelope and delivered it that afternoon.

A few days later, Mrs Day wrote a letter back to Lucy and Jane Jones and said that the Committee had decided to use the chutney money to buy all the decorations to make the village hall look really pretty for the party, and for some boxes of Christmas crackers, too, to put on each side plate at the dinner; and she asked if, nearer the time, Lucy and Jane Jones would like to come with her to Stillford, to help choose the decorations.

And, nearer the time, that was just what they did.

Lucy and Mark-by-the-pond got out the brick box.

THE CRIB BABY

One Friday afternoon, when it was very foggy and grey, and Lucy Billings was feeling cross because she had the end of a snuffly cold, a knock came at the kitchen door. When Mrs Billings went to open it, there stood Lucy's playgroup friend Mark-by-the-pond, with his mother and his sister Emily, who was three. And Lucy was very cheered up to see them, and Rosie the baby was cheered too, and kicked her legs and shouted and shouted, until Emily patted her and said, "There, there, baby," just like a real mother.

And while Lucy and Mark-by-the-pond got out the brick box so that they could build skyscraper buildings, Lucy's mother put the kettle on and found the cake tin, and Mark-by-the-pond's mother sat down at the big kitchen table. She said that it was very nice to be asked to stay for tea, but that what she had really come with was a problem. She said that she and Mr Field had been invited to a wedding the next day, in a city quite a long way off, and that they really did want to go, because it was Mrs Field's best-friend-from-schoolday's daughter who was getting married. And they had replied to say that they *would* go. But then they had found out that children were not to be allowed at the wedding because so many people would want to take them that there would be just *too* many altogether, and, as the people who were getting married couldn't very well choose just a few children to go, they had sent round a card saying they couldn't have any children at all.

"Well, that would have been fine, and we quite understood," Mrs Field said, "and Mrs Wood's Kathy was going to look after Mark and Emily for the day. But now we've just heard that she has the flu and is in bed, and can't come after all. Mark can go to Mark-down-the-lane's house; they have very kindly said that he can stay all day and for the night as well. But what about Emily?" And Emily, who was playing mothers and babies on the floor with Rosie, and trying to get her to eat pretending-cereal off a teaspoon, said, "Yes, what about Emily?" in a very waily sort of voice. So Lucy Billings's mother said, "What about you? Well, *you* will come and spend the day here with us, won't you?"

Then Emily jumped up and clapped and

danced about, and Rosie the baby laughed and clapped too, though of course she didn't understand what it was all about, she was just doing what Emily did. And then Emily said, "And bring a little bag with my toothbrush and pyjamas in, and stay the whole night?" Lucy's mother said yes, certainly, if Emily really wanted to and was grown-up enough, and Emily said that of course she certainly was. "I shall stay for all week and forever, I'm so grown-up-enough," she said.

Mrs Field asked if it was really all right and quite convenient, and Lucy's mother said it was perfectly all right, and would be great fun for Rosie to have Emily to stay. "And fun for Lucy, too," she said. She gave Lucy a very particular look, which Lucy knew meant that she was not to say anything otherwise. Because sometimes Emily

Field could be quite a naughty child, though she was never really *bad*-naughty.

"Where will Emily sleep?" Lucy asked them. Her mother said they'd think about that later, but probably in the little bed in Rosie's room, and Emily said, "Yes! Yes!" and jumped up and down again, and then she wanted to go upstairs right away, at once, to see the room and the little bed. So Lucy's mother took her, and Emily's mother and Rosie went too. But Lucy and Mark-by-the-pond stayed in the kitchen, building the skyscraper buildings in a very quiet and peaceful sort of way.

Now on the next day, when Emily was going to be staying for the whole day and night, other exciting things were happening too, and the most exciting thing was that it was the Saturday before Christmas. In fact, that whole week had been exciting already.

The playgroup Christmas party.

First of all, the playgroup had done a nativity play in the village hall, to which the mothers and fathers, as well as other visitors, had been invited, and Lucy Billings had been the innkeeper's wife and Jane Jones had been an angel, and they had done very well, without making any mistakes, and everybody had clapped and clapped. The next day there had been the playgroup Christmas party, with jellies to eat, and iced cakes and mince pies and crackers and balloons, and everybody had worn a paper crown and played games.

Then Lucy Billings and Jane Jones, with their mothers, had left Rosie the baby and brothers, Ben and Jack with their fathers, and gone into Stillford in the car after it was dark, to the late-night shopping in the centre of town. All the streets had been decorated with Christmas lights, in the shape of angels with shining silver wings and Christmas trees with glowing baubles, and the shops were like fairy caves, glittering with lights and stars and silver and gold, and piles of presents. And they had all gone to visit Father Christmas in the Ice Palace, which Lucy thought was the most beautiful place she had ever seen. Father Christmas had talked to them in a very jolly, friendly way, and asked them what presents they would like him to bring (though afterwards Lucy and Jane Jones decided that this shop Father Christmas was not the same one as the real-life, Christmas Eve one, and their mothers agreed, and said that he was an ordinary man, dressed up in Father Christmas clothes).

So it had been a very exciting, getting-ready-for-Christmas week altogether. The big kitchen table at Beehive Cottage had been full of mince pies and sausage rolls and Christmas cake, and the kitchen table at Old Leas Farmhouse, where Jane Jones lived, had been covered with special Christmas cards and gift tags and calendars and decorations that Mrs Jones made, and all sorts of parcels had arrived with the post lady, and mysteriously disappeared again at once. On Sunday, Lucy Billings and brother Ben were going to help their father get the roof-rack onto the car, and drive over to Little Miston to the farm that sold Christmas trees, and choose theirs, to bring home.

But on this Saturday, after Emily had arrived with her bag and taken it upstairs and put it beside the little bed in Rosie the baby's room, they all put on their coats and hats and scarves and gloves, because it was another very cold, grey and foggy day, and

There were piles and piles of holly branches with scarlet berries.

set off up the lane and along the High Street, to the gate that led to the church. Lucy's mother and Jane Jones' mother and some other ladies were going to be part of Mrs Potter's "decorating team" which meant that they would help fill the church with beautiful greenery and flowers and berries, all ready for Christmas.

And when they got there, most of the other ladies had already arrived, and in the middle of the church by the christening font, where there was plenty of space, were piles and piles of holly branches with scarlet berries, and long strandy bits of green ivy and branches of other dark green and yellowy-green leaves, and jars of fat white and yellow and purple chrysanthemums. There were also bunches and bundles of leaves and thistle heads and seed pods that were gold and silver, because Jane Jones' mother had sprayed them with special paint.

All the electric heaters inside the church had been switched on, but it was still a bit shivery-cold, so the children kept on their coats, gloves and scarves (but they took their hats off, because Lucy Billings's mother said that was what you should do in a church). Then, while the ladies were all being busy with the decorations, Lucy and Jane Jones took Rosie the baby and Jack by the hands, because they could both walk just a little, and showed them round the church. They climbed in and out of the seats and took the nice bright kneeler-pads off their hooks and piled them up like bricks, and then unpiled them again and sat down on them, like stools. And Emily had brought Lucy's old dolls' pram, which Lucy didn't play with much any more, and she was very happy indeed, just pushing it up and down and in and out and round and round the church, with her dolly Grace inside it. So, all in all, they had a very good time.

Then Mrs Day called to them to come and look what she was doing. When they went to the corner of the church they saw that she had two very large wooden boxes, and that she was getting things out of them and unwrapping them, from old pieces of torn sheet, and she asked Lucy and Jane Jones if they would like to help her, provided they were very, very careful, because she said that the things inside the boxes were very old, older even than Mrs Tabb, and fragile – which meant that they could break easily.

And when they carefully unwrapped and unwrapped, and pulled off the old pieces of sheet, Lucy and Jane Jones found all the figures that went into the Christmas crib, made out of beautiful old painted-plaster stuff. Besides Mary and Joseph and the wise men and the shepherds and two angels with wings, there was a donkey, a cow, a sheep with a lamb, a goat, and a very small dog.

Mrs Day had brought a plastic sack full of clean straw from the farm, and they helped her to spread it out around and under the wooden stable and the manger and then to set the figures carefully, carefully in their places. And all the time, Rosie the baby and Jack watched, sitting in their buggies, because Lucy Billings' mother had said they were better strapped in again just now, "out of harm's way", while the crib was being set up. But Emily was trundling round and round and in and out and up and down with the dolls' pram, and didn't come near them

Emily trundled round and round and in and out and up and down with the dolls' pram.

once, only sang and talked to herself, and to her dolly Grace, until they had almost completely finished. Then she did come, and stood and looked, and said in a clear little voice,

"But there is *no* baby Jesus!"

And Mrs Day explained that there was but that he stayed wrapped up in the wooden box until Christmas morning, when he would be taken out and put in the manger. "Because that is the day he was born," she said.

"Yes," said Emily, "Christmas Day is his birthday."

But then she said that she wanted to see the baby Jesus doll even so, and her voice began to get very cross and whiny, so Mrs Day said that she would unwrap the figure, and they could all have just a peep. So they crowded round and saw the plaster baby

Jesus, lying in his piece of old sheet, with his arms stretched out, and he looked quite like an ordinary, small, real baby, only more smiley, and with a bit chipped off his nose.

And Emily put out a little finger and stroked his cheek and smiled back at him, and was very, very interested, and helped Mrs Day wrap him back in his sheet and lay him carefully in the wooden box again.

Then one of the ladies called that there were drinks for everybody, and there was a table set up at the back, by the notice board, with Thermos flasks full of hot coffee and chocolate, and beakers of orange for the children, and a plate of mince pies and shortbread biscuits too. So they all gathered round and had a church picnic, and admired the decorations. There were green leaves and red berries and chrysanthemums and gold and silver branches, on all the window-ledges and the altar steps, and around the pulpit and the christening font, and in big stone jars on the altar table. Later that night, some of the ladies were to come back and decorate the Christmas tree, when it had arrived and been set in place.

But Emily wouldn't come to the table and have a drink and a mince pie, she stayed by herself at the other end of the church, with the old dolls' pram, and Lucy Billings' mother said it would be best just to let her be, as she was "a child with a mind of her own".

Just before they left, Lucy Billings and Jane Jones went quietly back to the corner where the crib was, and looked at the beautiful, still figures kneeling and the animals standing beside the empty manger, which was all ready and waiting for the baby Jesus, and Lucy felt a very happy and

Just before they left, Lucy Billings and Jane Jones went quietly back to the corner where the crib was.

excited feeling suddenly fizz up inside her, because now it was nearly, *very* nearly, Christmas.

Then they all went home, and it was quite dark, but the foggy greyness had gone and the moon and stars had come out, and the wheels of the two buggies and of the old dolls' pram went trundle-trundle down the lane.

At the front gate of the house next door, they said goodnight to Jane Jones and her mother and Jack, who was fast asleep, and went up the front path and into Beehive Cottage, where Lucy's father and brother Ben were waiting. And they all had sausages and chips and treacle tart for supper, and Emily played with Rosie the baby. Later on, they had a bath together, which was great fun and a lot of noise and splashing for both of them, but nobody was a bit cross or bad-tempered or silly the whole evening.

But after Rosie the baby had gone to bed, and just a little while after that, Emily had gone too, and been tucked up in her little bed and kissed goodnight and read to, and after she had said that she liked it here so much she thought she would like to bring the rest of her clothes and toys and *live* at Beehive Cottage, and after she and Rosie the baby had both fallen fast asleep – well, then a very, very funny and surprising thing happened.

Mrs Billings was tidying up, and she said, "Lucy, would you be a good girl and bring in that old pram from the hallway, and I'll put it back in the shed later?" So Lucy did. And when she got the pram into the kitchen, she thought she ought to take Emily's old dolly Grace out of it, in case that got put away in the shed too, because

Lucy bent down and pulled back the bit of old quilt that was the pram cover.

Emily would be sure to want it when she got home. (Though she hadn't wanted to take Grace to bed with her, she only wanted her pink squirrel. "Grace must stay in her pram and be asleep," she had told Lucy's mother.)

So now, Lucy bent down and pulled back the bit of old quilt that was the pram cover, and there she saw Grace the dolly. And also SOMETHING ELSE. She saw, lying beside Grace, a bit squashed in and half wrapped up in a piece of old sheet, *the baby Jesus doll from the church crib*!

"Oh look, look! Come and see what Emily has brought home in the pram!" Lucy said, and her mother, and brother Ben came. They all stared and stared, and for a moment none of them said anything at all. But Lucy had a very funny feeling inside, because she wondered what would happen, and if Emily had really meant to *take* the baby Jesus doll. But then her mother said, "Oh dear, oh dear!"

"But," said Lucy, "we shall have to take it back."

"Oh, of course we shall, I'll take it back first thing in the morning. I'll just pop it back into the box, that would be the best."

"And won't you tell anyone?" Lucy asked.

But her mother said that no, she wouldn't, because really, Emily was only just three years old and didn't quite understand what she had done, Mrs Billings was sure.

So that was what happened. Lucy's mother slipped up to the church very early the next morning, before the first service, and put the baby Jesus doll back, and nobody ever knew it had been away.

But a little later on, when Emily's mother and father arrived at Beehive Cottage to collect Emily, and she was saying thank you for having me and going home with her little case, Lucy Billings ran and fetched the doll Grace.

"Look, you nearly forgot her," she said to Emily. "*She was in my old pram.*"

And she looked very hard at Emily, and Emily looked very hard back at her, and they went on looking for quite a long minute. But then Lucy saw her mother making a frowny sort of face over Emily's shoulder, and she knew that the frowny face meant that she was not to say *anything at all* about what had happened while Emily's mother and father had been away at the wedding.

So she didn't.

THE
END

ZENOBIA AND MOUSE

Vivian French

In many ways Zenobia is a quite ordinary, lively little girl. She goes to school, she likes making mess, she doesn't much like baths and, of course, she has a best friend. But Zenobia's best friend is very special. His name is Mouse and he has a tail, a furry body, tattered pink ears, button eyes that shine and wink – and, most extraordinary of all, he talks!

These six acutely observed and wryly amusing stories are ideal for reading aloud at bedtime or any other storytime.

FRIENDS NEXT DOOR

Susan Hill

Lucy Billings is a small girl who lives with her family in Beehive Cottage in Codling Village. In these three stories to read aloud, Lucy gets a new friend next door, she joins in a cat search and she and the rest of the village are snowed in!

"Hill excels in these tales from the everyday life of a small girl in a Cotswoldy village."
The Guardian

"Beautifully written ... equally suitable for solo reading or for reading out loud."
The School Librarian